MESSAGES FROM BEYOND

STEPHANIE WATSON

NIGHT FALL

MESSAGES FROM BEYOND

STEPHANIE WATSON

MINNEAPOLIS

Darby Creek
A division of Lerner Publishing Group, Inc.
241 First Avenue North
Minneapolis, MN 55401 U.S.A.

Website address: www.lernerbooks.com

Cover design: Becky Daum
Cover photograph: Stephan Zabel/iStockphoto

Watson, Stephanie, 1969–
Messages from beyond / by Stephanie Watson.
   p.   cm. — (Night fall)
ISBN 978-0-7613-6146-6 (lib. bdg. : alk. paper)
[1. Horror stories.] I. Title.
PZ7.W32949Me 2010
[Fic]—dc22   2010003316

Manufactured in the United States of America
1–BP–7/15/10

To my son, Jake.
No matter how many books I
write, you will always be my
greatest creation.

*Deep into that darkness peering, long I stood there
   wondering, fearing,
Doubting, dreaming dreams no mortal ever dared
   to dream before*

—*Edgar Allan Poe,* The Raven

Cassie walked along the path from school, her books weighing heavily in her arms. Her feet stomped out the familiar rhythm home, but her mind was far away. What should she wear to Bridgewater High's Halloween Havoc party this year? Sexy vampire, or Lady Gaga? Tough call. Her mother would probably nix the Lady Gaga idea as too bizarre, and she'd have to keep Vampira relatively G-rated.

Maybe she could cover up her costume with her coat until she got out the door. She'd probably need one anyway. It could get cold on Halloween in Bridgewater. Last year the temperature had dipped nearly to freezing. Just remembering last Halloween was enough to make her shiver.

Actually, she was shivering for real. It was getting cold. Goosebumps popped up along her arms and legs.

It was also getting foggy. Tendrils of white curled around her feet, sending a chill from her ankles to the top of her head and making her hair stand on end. Cassie stopped walking. Hadn't it just been sunny and warm a minute ago?

The street in front of her was starting to look a lot like that horror movie *The Fog* her Dad had rented from Netflix a couple of years ago. She'd snickered through the whole thing, but she'd really lost it during the fog attack that killed a bunch of people. That fog was about as scary as marshmallow fluff.

This was *not* that fog. This fog slowly rose up, surrounding everything. Now the sidewalk was completely gone. In another minute, so were her legs. Everything around her just disappeared into the gray blankness.

"Okay, this is freaking me out a little," Cassie said out loud. Her voice echoed around her. She looked frantically to her left and right, trying to pick out any familiar shape. She couldn't see a thing.

Then a shadow approached. Cassie caught her breath as it grew bigger and bigger. Whatever the shadow was, it was closing in on her.

"Wait a minute," Cassie said to herself as the shadow's owner came into focus. She sighed in relief. It was just a kid. She didn't recognize him, but he looked like he was about her age.

He was wearing a jean jacket with a button-down gray shirt underneath. He kind of looked like that guy Robert Pattinson, the sexy actor from the vampire movies.

He was giving her a crooked smile. Normally, she'd be tripping over her feet and stumbling over her words if a guy even glanced her way. This time she managed to smile back.

He came closer, stopping just inches away from her. He didn't say a word but reached out and gently touched her cheek. Cassie shivered again, but this time it wasn't from the cold mist. She didn't even know this guy, but for some reason she didn't care.

He whispered, "Cassie . . . I missed you." She closed her eyes.

Something was wrong. Cassie could sense it. The soft hand on her face had turned hard. It was scratching like nails at her skin. The voice too—it didn't sound human. It sounded low and whispery, like death.

Cassie forced herself to open her eyes. There, standing where the boy had been, was a monstrous creature. Its head was a skull with bits of rotten flesh clinging to it. Its long white claws were wrapped around her face, squeezing her. More gnarled fingers were reaching around her body, squeezing tighter and tighter.

The creature leaned toward her. Cassie felt its sour breath lapping at her face. The creature opened its mouth for a kiss.

Cassie screamed. She bolted upright in bed, her arms flailing everywhere. Her skin was still stinging where the creature had grabbed her in her dream. Her clothes were damp and rumpled against her skin. Her breath came in short, fast gasps.

She must have fallen asleep while doing her homework. But if it had just been a dream, why hadn't the howling stopped?

Duh. It was the Halloween ringtone she'd

just downloaded to her phone. She frantically grabbed for the phone under the mound of covers and papers on her bed.

"Hello . . . hello?"

"Hey, Cassie! Cassie? What's wrong? Why are you breathing like that?"

"Oh hi, Jen." Cassie tried to catch her breath. "Sorry, I just woke up from a nap. What's going on?"

"Were you running a marathon in your dreams?"

"No, I just had a weird nightmare. I met this guy, but then he turned into this skeleton-monster creature that tried to kiss me."

"Ewww. Well, look on the bright side. At least a guy wanted to kiss you."

"Funny. So, what's up?"

"Well, I have some good news . . . and some bad news." Cassie's best friend had a habit of introducing topics with "I have some good news and some bad news." The good news was usually not good enough to balance out whatever major bummer she was about to throw Cassie's way.

"What is it now?" Cassie tried to hide the annoyance in her voice. Jen really did mean well.

"Well, I just got off the phone with Lisa, who got a text from Sami, who read in an e-mail from Emily that . . . someone is planning to ask you to Halloween Havoc."

That was the good news. Now for the bad news. "Who is it?"

"Jonah."

Jonah? The kid whose mother picked out his clothes for him? The guy who couldn't say a complete sentence to her without blushing and stammering? *He* was asking her to the party? Ugh. This was even worse than her crazy skeleton dream.

"Are you sure?" Cassie pressed, hoping that Jen's well-connected social network was wrong this one time.

"Totally sure. He told Max, and then Max texted Jon, and then—"

"I get it. So, what should I do? How do I say no to him when I don't have another date to the party?"

"I'd say you'd better get a date—quickly—so you have an excuse."

"Great advice," Cassie replied sarcastically. "I'll just open my BlackBerry and run down the list of all the guys who've been dying to ask me out, and . . ." There was a double beep on the line. "Wait. Someone is trying to text me. It might be my mom. She said she's coming home late from work tonight, and she gets annoyed with me if I don't answer her texts seconds later. Let me call you right back."

She hit the red button and went into her inbox.

Hey you. Where were you after school?

The number definitely wasn't her mom's. Was she supposed to have met someone after school?

Who is this? she quickly typed.

A minute later, she had another message.

You're funny. I liked the blue sweater today. You looked wicked awesome.

Wicked awesome? That was something her mother sometimes said. Cassie teased her mom about being stuck in 1985 whenever she said it.

Seriously. Who r u?

A few minutes later: *Ethan. Did you forget me already? Nice spelling, by the way.*

Cassie quickly typed: *Sorry. You have the wrong person.*

She dialed Jen back. "Who was it from?" Jen asked.

"Some guy named Ethan. He had the wrong number. I knew it wasn't for me when he wrote that I looked 'wicked awesome' today."

Jen laughed. "Must have been one of your mom's friends."

Cassie's phone beeped again. "Let me call you back. I don't think this guy is getting the hint that I'm not the person he's looking for."

Are you mad at me?

How can I be mad at you when I don't know you? Cassie typed angrily.

Cassie—it's me. Ethan.

WHO R U? Cassie pounded at the tiny keys, nearly breaking her brand-new phone.

A picture started appearing on the screen. As it emerged, Cassie could see rumpled hair and blue eyes. The picture looked familiar. He looked just like the guy from her dream.

What's wrong with you today? You're so flaky." Jen was steering Cassie down the hall toward the locker room. Their gym teacher, Mrs. Wilson, had zero tolerance for lateness. A whistle always bounced on her ample chest, and she wasn't afraid to use it. Anyone who dared come to gym even a few minutes late got the whistle—and the detention that came with it.

"I'm just thinking about that Ethan guy who texted me. It's so weird that his picture looked exactly like the guy in that nightmare I had yesterday."

"I'm sure it was just a bizarre coincidence. Are you sneaking into your mom's Halloween stash again? Maybe it was a sugar-fueled hallucination."

"My mom hides the stash. She knows I'm a total pig around chocolate." Cassie snorted for effect. "How do you think he knew my name?"

"No idea. Maybe you've got a secret admirer." Jen quickly changed into her gym uniform and was now looking at herself in the mirror. Cassie came up to her and put an arm around her shoulder. Could two best friends look more different? Jen always looked perfect. Perfect body, perfect blonde hair. Cassie used to be so jealous of Jen in middle school. But now Cassie kind of liked her own hippie look: curly auburn hair frizzing out in every direction, dark liner along her big eyes, long earrings. She made it work.

From inside her gym locker, Cassie's bag vibrated.

"Ooh, I'm telling! You're not allowed to bring cell phones in here." Jen lifted an invisible whistle to her mouth and blew. "Detention, young lady!"

"Shut up," Cassie whispered. "It's on vibrate. I can't cut off my mother—she'll lose it if she can't reach me every second of the day."

There was a text message. *Meet me at 3, outside by the flagpole. I brought Catcher in the Rye. Thought you'd read it with me.*

"Who is it?" Jen leaned over to get a look at the screen. "Is it *him*?"

"Yeah. How'd he know *The Catcher in the Rye* is my favorite book?"

"Maybe he's been following you."

"Do you know anyone at school named Ethan?"

"No, but he could be using a fake name. Maybe it's Jonah, trying to get inside your head."

"Please don't say that." Cassie rolled her eyes. "Anyway, Jonah's mother won't let him have a cell phone. Remember? She thinks that texting leads straight to the devil."

The phone buzzed again. *Will you come? I really need to talk to you.* Then, a few seconds later: *Holden is phony.*

"Who's that?" Jen asked.

"Holden Caulfield, from *The Catcher in the Rye*," Cassie replied. "Holden calls everything phony, but he's the one who's an unreliable narrator."

"He took the time to learn your favorite book. He can't be all that bad," Jen said.

More buzzing. *Please.*

I'll be there, she typed. She definitely needed to nip this wannabe stalker in the bud.

I t was 3:15. Cassie crossed her arms more tightly. Her jean jacket wasn't even coming close to keeping her warm enough. *Five more minutes and I'm out of here,* she thought. She paced around the flagpole, trying to look as though she had a reason to be there and wasn't getting stood up by some guy she didn't even know—or want to know.

Oh no. Jen was right. Jonah was heading her way. He was wearing a mom-issue short-sleeve, button-down shirt and khakis and trying to look casual while balancing a stack of books under one arm.

"Hi, Cassie." When he smiled, his braces flashed. Jonah was the only senior who still wore braces. He'd gotten them late because his mother believed that altering one's appearance was messing with God's natural creation. But Jonah had convinced her that having straight teeth would help him get into a better college.

"Oh . . . hi, Jonah." Cassie tried to hide the disappointment in her voice.

"I . . . um . . . I . . ."

It was funny that Jonah stumbled so much when he tried to talk to her. He was about the only guy in school who didn't make her stumble over her own words.

"Listen, Jonah. It was really sweet of you to ask me here, but . . ."

He squinted. "Huh? I—I didn't . . ." Then a smile spread over his face. "Were we supposed to meet?"

Cassie realized her mistake. "I'm sorry, Jonah—I was confused there for a second."

Jonah showing up here must have been a coincidence, Cassie thought. He looked too surprised to have been the one who texted her.

"I—I really have been wanting to talk to you, though," Jonah said quickly. "Do you have a minute?"

Cassie shook her head, immediately feeling horrible when she registered Jonah's hurt expression. "I'm sorry, Jonah, but I'm meeting someone. He should be here any second." She emphasized the word *he.*

"Oh." He looked at the ground. "Well, maybe we can talk some other time."

Jonah shuffled off, his eyes still glued to his shoes. Cassie watched his slumped shape grow smaller and smaller until he turned the corner. He actually wasn't that bad-looking. His long brown hair fell over one eye in a way that might have been appealing, if you could get past the braces and his awkward way. *At least Jonah*

would have showed up when he promised, she
thought glumly.

Her cell phone vibrated. She'd forgotten to
put the ringer back on after gym class.

Where are you?

"What do you mean, where am I?" she
yelled pointlessly at her phone's tiny screen.
"Where are *you?*"

A few kids who were walking by turned to
stare at Cassie. She quickly put the phone to her
ear and pretended to be deep in conversation.
When the kids had passed, she put the phone
back down and typed furiously—*I'm at the
flagpole in front of Bridgewater High. Where the
heck are you?*

A few seconds later, her phone buzzed. *I'm
right here.*

I don't know what game he thinks he's playing, but I am NOT going to waste my time chasing after this idiot!" She slammed the front door. Cassie knew she was talking to herself, but she didn't care. She had stood in front of that stupid flagpole for nearly half an hour in the freezing cold—for nothing.

"Who's playing what game?" Cassie's mother walked into the living room, balancing a stack of papers in one hand and a coffee mug in the other. Joanne Lewis was lead accountant for Rex Accounting, and her company allowed her to be on a flex-time schedule. That meant she was often home early to keep an eye on Cassie.

"Oh, it's nothing. Just some kid at school is messing with me."

"Who is it?" Her mom frowned, revealing deepening lines in her forehead. *If she keeps worrying like this, Mom's going to need one big shot of Botox,* Cassie thought.

"I don't know. He says his name is Ethan, but I don't know anyone named Ethan at Bridgewater." Now her mother's eyes darkened slightly. "He keeps sending me texts. Today he asked me to meet him at the flagpole after school and never showed up, but he texted me that he was there."

"How do you know this is a student, Cassandra? This could be some creepy middle-aged guy who's gotten hold of your cell phone number." She sighed. "I told your father he had no business getting you a cell phone. You're way too young."

"I doubt it. I just got the phone, and hardly anyone knows my number. It's probably one of the guys in my homeroom who are always giving me a hard time. Maybe they grabbed my phone while I was away from my desk and took the number from it."

Her mother didn't look convinced. "Well, if you see that number come up again, don't respond, okay? And let me know right away if he doesn't stop texting."

"I will. Anyway, I'm done with Ethan— whoever he is."

"Good. Listen, go upstairs and get your homework done. I've got to finish crunching these numbers for Joneston Motors." She waved the big pile of papers in her hand. "This new client is driving me nuts. They just sent me these files today, and they want the whole spreadsheet done by tomorrow. Dinner will be a little late, but I'll make something special—okay?"

"Sure, Mom."

Cassie headed upstairs. As soon as she had plopped down on her still-unmade bed, her phone started vibrating again. She just let it buzz.

⁓

Cassie didn't remember leaving her window open, but as night settled in she could feel the wind blowing in through the sheer curtains. Even underneath her thick covers, Cassie shivered. She slid out of bed and went to close the window.

Behind the open window there was a face. It was him—Ethan. How did he know where she lived?

"Hi, Cassie," he said, smiling at her. "Where were you today? I missed you."

"Why didn't you show up?" she demanded. "I waited for you."

"I was there, Cassie." More of that sweet

smile. "Don't you know I'm always there for you?"

Her anger faded. There was something so understanding about the way he looked at her.

"It's okay. We must have just missed each other. Do you want to come in?" she asked. "Here, climb in off that ladder."

She leaned her head slightly out the window. Then she realized—there was no ladder. Her bedroom was on the second floor. Ethan was outside her window. He wasn't holding onto anything.

For the second time in two days, Cassie woke up screaming.

I got five more text messages from him last night. I ignored them at first, but he didn't give up, so I started to respond. It's weird. He acts like he's known me forever. He knows my favorite foods, my favorite books. He's really easy to talk to."

"Maybe he's a stalker," suggested Lisa, who was sitting across from Cassie at their usual lunch table. "It could be that sleazy new English teacher, Mr. Aspic. He's always leering at us.

He would definitely know his literature, at least."

"Okay, that's just disgusting," Jen cut in, sending Lisa a dirty look. "Has Ethan ever actually called you?"

"No."

"Have you ever tried to call his number?"

"Yes, a few times. It just rings and rings."

"He says he goes to Bridgewater, right?"

"Yes. He told me he has Mr. Simmons for calculus and someone named Miss Flowers for English, but I've never heard of her, have you?"

"Um-hum," Lisa mumbled through a mouthful of chicken salad. "I think my mom had a Miss Flowers when she went here. She said she always got her notes confiscated in that class."

"Why don't you wait outside Mr. Simmons's class for Ethan today? That's last period," Jen suggested.

"Good idea." Maybe today would be the day Cassie could find out once and for all who was texting her.

Cassie managed to sneak her way out of her last-period history class a few minutes early, feigning a stomachache. She took off for Mr. Simmons's class, which was all the way on the other side of the school.

She wasn't quick enough. As she ran down the second-floor hallway, doors started to open. Students streamed out, heading for their lockers. Just going forward was like moving through an obstacle course. Cassie narrowly missed crashing headfirst into Matt Longacre, the captain of the soccer team. She wasn't so lucky when Jonah crossed her path.

The next thing she knew, she was on the floor looking up at him.

"I am so sorry, Cassie. I d-didn't see you there!" he stammered.

"It's not your fault, Jonah." Cassie rubbed the back of her head where it had smacked the floor.

"Are you okay?"

"Yeah, I'm fine. I shouldn't have been running. I forgot what a total klutz I am."

"Yeah, me too." Jonah reached out and helped pull her up. For having such scrawny arms, he was actually pretty strong.

Cassie stood there for a few seconds, not sure what to say. "Well, I'm late. I've got to go. Sorry for running into you."

"It's okay." He looked at the ceiling, as if searching for the right words. "Um, Cassie? I'd still love to talk to you if you've got some time."

"I'm kind of in a rush right now. Maybe later, okay?"

"Sure."

She hated to leave him with that sad-puppy look, but she didn't want to miss Ethan.

Cassie got to Mr. Simmons's room just in time to see the last two girls walking out. She was too late.

"Mr. Simmons?" she asked hesitantly as she entered the room. He was sitting at his desk, grading papers.

"Yes." He looked up over his black-rimmed glasses at her. "Can I help you?"

"I was looking for someone."

"Aren't we all," he said, smiling at his own joke. "Who are you looking for?"

"His name's Ethan. I'm not sure of his last name. Do you have anyone named Ethan in your class?"

"I've had many Ethans in here over the years, but sorry—this year isn't one of them."

"Oh."

"You look puzzled," Mr. Simmons said. "Can I help?"

"It's just that someone supposedly named Ethan told me he was in your class."

"Maybe he meant Mr. Sawyers's class? The students are always getting our names confused." He shrugged as if to say, *kids—go figure.*

"I'll try him. Thanks."

Instead, Cassie headed for the library. Ethan didn't say what year he was, but she figured he had to be either a junior or senior to have Mr. Simmons or Mr. Sawyers for math. Unless Ethan was new at the school, there had to be a record of him in last year's yearbook.

After knocking nearly all the yearbooks off the shelf (and getting a raised eyebrow from Miss Woods, the librarian), Cassie pulled down the last two years' editions and thumbed through them. Nothing. The only Ethan had been a freshman last year, but his family had moved to Poughkeepsie last summer. She put the yearbooks back and decided to try the school office.

Elise Jenkins was there as usual, typing away at what was probably the only real typewriter left in existence. Elise had been a friend of her mom's at Bridgewater back in the mid-1980s. After graduation, Elise hadn't gotten very far. She had earned a degree in communications at Noble College. Then, as Cassie's mom said, Elise "undervalued her own potential" by getting an administrative job in the Bridgewater High School office. Something sad had happened to Elise, although Cassie wasn't sure what. But it had brought Elise back home after college.

"Hi, Elise!" Cassie called out, trying to sound cheerful.

"Well, hello, sweetie!" Elise jumped up from her typewriter and came around the desk to envelop Cassie in a big, Halloween-sweatered hug. Elise had a sweater for every occasion. Christmas, Halloween, Easter—Veteran's Day, even. This one featured an assortment of pumpkins.

"How are you doing? Is everything okay?" She pulled back and fixed Cassie with a concerned look.

"Everything's fine."

"Is your mom okay? Not working too hard crunching those numbers?"

"Nope. Mom's fine too."

"Well, what's up?"

"I have a bit of a favor to ask. I'm looking for someone."

"Is it a boy?" Elise smiled mischievously.

"Actually, yes. His name's Ethan. I don't know his last name, but he told me he was in Mr. Simmons's calculus class. He texted me a picture of himself. He's got blue eyes and brown hair that kind of sticks up in a James Dean sort of way." She figured Elise wouldn't get the Robert Pattinson reference.

A strange look passed over Elise's eyes. "Did you say 'Ethan'?" she asked.

"Yes. What is it?"

"Nothing . . . . Not if he sent you a text message." She shook her head quickly. "Are you sure someone isn't trying to play a trick on you? Or maybe someone has a crush on you." Elise grinned knowingly.

"Not likely. The only boy who currently likes me isn't allowed to have a cell phone. So, do you think you might be able to look him up by first name only?"

"I'll poke around in the school archives—see what I can find."

"Thanks, Elise. You're the best." She gave her mom's friend another quick hug.

"Now get home before your mother starts worrying."

Cassie was just lifting a forkful of mashed potatoes when her phone began vibrating.

"Cassandra, how many times have I told you to leave the phone upstairs while we're eating? Dinnertime is not the time for talking on the phone. It's too much of a distraction." Funny that her mother should rag on her for dinnertime distractions, when she had a pile of spreadsheets stacked up next to her plate.

"Sorry. I had it on vibrate." Cassie looked down at the screen. Ethan again.

Today was a rough day. Sometimes I feel like no one gets me. I think you're the only one who understands.

Cassie quickly shoved the phone under the table.

"Who was it?" her mother asked. Cassie shoveled the mashed potatoes into her mouth. "Was it that Ethan guy again? Is he still harassing you?"

"Who's Ethan?" Her father lowered his *New York Times* to look at her inquisitively.

"No one, Dad. Someone supposedly with that name has been texting me. I'm sure it's just a prank."

"Do you have this guy's phone number?" her mom asked. "I don't like this one bit. I think it's time we trace the number and get the police involved."

Cassie rolled her eyes. "Mom, it's fine. It's got to be someone at school, because no one else would have known my name. Like I said, hardy anyone knows my number."

"And it will stay that way, if I have anything to say about it. You're my only child, and I'm going to do everything in my power to keep you safe."

Being an only child had its advantages, but one of the biggest disadvantages was the overprotective parent syndrome. Her mother had barely let her out of her sight during the last seventeen years.

"Mom, I promise I'll come straight to you if I'm at all worried that this is anything but another kid at school having some fun at my expense."

Her mother didn't look convinced, but she reluctantly let the topic go—for now.

The next day, Cassie and Jen were making their way to the cafeteria for lunch. As they passed the school office, Cassie heard her name. She stopped and popped her head into the office.

"Do you have a second?" Elise was standing near the door with a strange look on her face. "I found someone, but . . ." She shook her head briskly. "I'm sure it's not who you're looking for."

Elise led Cassie over to her desk, where a yearbook was sitting open. "This was the only Ethan I could find who matched your description," she said, pointing to a picture of a senior.

Cassie sucked in her breath. It was him. *Ethan Davis.* He was wearing a jean jacket with a patch on the arm that read "The Cure." He had the same blue eyes—the same cockeyed grin—as the guy in her dream and on her cell phone.

"That's him. That's the guy who's been texting me."

Elise looked up at her sharply. "Cassie, it can't be."

"Why not?"

Elise closed the yearbook. On the cover, in gold lettering, it read "1985." "It can't be him . . . because Ethan Davis died in a car accident twenty-five years ago."

Jen pulled on a pair of black patent-leather boots over her black jeans. "Punk enough?"

Cassie surveyed her friend's ripped black T-shirt and pink-sprayed hair. "Even as Sid Vicious you look hot," she said, smiling.

On the bed, Cassie's phone started playing "Use Somebody" by Kings of Leon.

"It's your dead boyfriend again," Jen said.

"Not funny." Cassie shivered. "I need to find out who's messing with me. My mother is about to call in a SWAT team and have every creepy forty-year-old guy in Bridgewater arrested."

"That's the benefit of being an only child. Twenty-four-hour supervision."

The phone beeped, signaling that a text message had come in. Cassie glanced at it but didn't pick up the message.

"Who do you think it could be?" Jen asked, helping Cassie adjust her vampire wig. "Is anyone ticked off at you?"

"I'm not the most popular girl in school, but I don't think I've done anything to deserve that kind of revenge." Cassie pressed false eyelashes onto her right eyelid.

"How about Emma London? Remember last year when you called her out for cheating on that U.S. history test?"

"She got over it. We just went to the movies last weekend."

There was a knock on Cassie's bedroom door.

"Come in!" she yelled.

Her mother peeked in, then opened the door fully and looked Cassie up and down disapprovingly. "You need to pull that skirt down." Cassie did as she was told, knowing full well that she'd pull it back up as soon as they got to the Halloween party.

From the bed, the phone beeped again. Her mother's eyes darted to it.

"Please tell me you're not getting texts from that Ethan guy again," she said, her eyebrows raised.

Jen grabbed the phone. "That's just Steve. He needed directions to your house to come pick us up."

"Okay." Cassie's mom didn't look convinced. "Make sure you're home by midnight, and keep your phone with you at all times so I can reach you. Oh, and make sure this Steve guy drives safely. Absolutely NO alcohol. If he drinks, I drive you home. Got it?"

"Sure, Mom." Cassie kissed her mother on the cheek reassuringly.

Her mother looked Cassie up and down once more and shook her head, smiling. "Have fun, but be careful tonight." She wagged a finger at Cassie and then backed out of the room, shutting the door behind her.

"Do you want to know what the text said?" Jen was still holding the phone.

"Not really, but shoot."

"It said, 'Come over.'"

"Hey, Cassie! How was the Halloween party?" Elise called out as Cassie walked through the doorway of the school office. Now that Halloween was over, Elise had already started on her collection of Thanksgiving sweaters. Today's showcased a big, smiling turkey. Cassie doubted that any turkeys would have reason to smile on Thanksgiving.

"It was okay," she shrugged.

Cassie had spent practically the whole night

dodging Jonah. He wouldn't leave her side, and the sight of him as a giant banana threatened to send her into a giggle fit.

"So—I was wondering. About that guy Ethan," Cassie said, as Elise got noticeably paler. "Do you happen to know if his mom still lives in Bridgewater?"

"Why would you want to know that?" Elise looked even more worried.

"I just thought, maybe this person who is texting me as Ethan has some connection to the family. And maybe I can find out who it is by talking to Ethan's mom."

"I know Mrs. Davis was absolutely heartbroken after Ethan died. He was an only child—she never had any more kids, either. Then her husband died a few years later. They used to live in that purple-shuttered house on Sable Road, right by Lake Pinquot. But I'm sure she's long gone by now."

"I know where that is. Thanks, Elise!"

"Sure, hon. But, like I said, Ethan's mother probably doesn't live there anymore."

"I know. I just want to check it out—just in case."

"Well, just don't go there alone. And make sure your mom knows where you're going."

"Absolutely." The little white lies were coming easier and easier these days.

Steve pulled his white Mustang to the curb
in front of a huge, gabled house with purple
shutters. "Is this it?" In sight just past the house
were the wooded shores of Lake Pinquot. Most
of the kids in town had gone there at least once
on a school field trip to study the waterfowl,
otters, beavers, and other local wildlife. And
all of them had heard at least one scary story
about the haunted-looking house at the edge of
the lake.

Cassie nodded.

"Pretty spooky," Steve continued. "I heard some old lady stabbed her husband sixteen times in there."

"Those are just stories. The house has a lot of character," Cassie insisted, but she shivered nonetheless. "You guys wait here. I'll be back in a few minutes."

"Are you sure you don't want us to come with you? There might be some wacko living there now," Jen said.

"Yeah, like that nutso old lady who offed her husband," Steve added, making a stabbing motion with one fist.

"I'll be fine. Just wait for me."

"We'll be here." Steve slipped his arm around Jen's shoulders. "I'll keep her occupied until you get back."

Jen rolled her eyes at him before turning back to Cassie. "Just be careful, okay? You have your cell phone. Call me if there's any problem."

"Promise." Cassie slammed the car door

behind her and made her way up the stone path.

The yard was a mess. Weeds were growing everywhere, over the path and up the steps to the front door. The door looked like it had been pretty impressive in its day—it was at least seven feet tall, with thick panes of stained glass on either side. But now the dark paint had faded, the stained glass was smudged with dirt, and the wood was peeling off in huge strips.

Cassie lifted the door knocker, which was shaped like a lion's head, and released it. She could hear the loud knock echoing inside the house.

There was no answer. Maybe the house was abandoned?

Just as Cassie was about to turn around and head back to Steve's car, she heard a tiny rustle from inside. A distorted face appeared in the stained glass. Then the door opened.

There stood a tiny woman with messy, gray-streaked hair. She was dressed in an old, stained sweatshirt and jeans. Cassie could tell that, like the house, this woman must also have been impressive in her day. It looked as if the years had taken their toll on her, though. Age and sorrow had left a web of wrinkles around her blue eyes and a downturn to her mouth.

As soon as the woman set eyes on Cassie, though, her frown turned into a beaming smile, and she gasped with pleasure.

Cassie took her response as a promising sign. "Hi . . . um, I'm Cassie. I'm a student at Bridgewater High. I was looking for Mrs. Davis?"

"*I'm* Liz Davis," the woman said happily, motioning to herself. "Please, please come in. I can't tell you how happy I am to see you!"

Cassie gave one quick wave to the car at the curb before following Mrs. Davis through the entryway and into a large living room. The furniture was covered in plastic, just as it was in Cassie's grandmother's house.

"Please, sit down," Mrs. Davis said,

motioning to the couch. "I'll get us something to drink."

The sofa made a loud squeaking sound as Cassie sat down on it. While she listened to Mrs. Davis rummaging around in the kitchen, she glanced around the room. It reminded her of a museum. It looked like nothing had been touched in years. In front of the couch, a vase sat in the middle of a large, dark-wood coffee table. The vase held a dead bunch of roses. The table, vase, and roses were all covered in a thick layer of dust.

Mrs. Davis bustled back in carrying a tray of tea and sugar cookies. "All I could find is chamomile tea. But you like that, don't you?" Actually, Cassie hated tea of all kinds, but she didn't want to be impolite.

"Sure. That's perfect," she said, hoping her smile looked sincere.

"These cookies were Ethan's favorites," Mrs. Davis said, looking up to stare at a point somewhere on the ceiling. She sighed heavily.

After they had added sugar and milk to their tea, Mrs. Davis plopped down on the sofa next to Cassie. "Look at you," she whispered, shaking her head. "It's so good to see you."

I t's, uh . . . it's nice to see you, too, Mrs. Davis,"
Cassie replied uneasily. "Actually, I'm here
to ask you about Ethan. I've been getting some
strange text messages recently . . ."

"My Ethan. I miss him so much," Mrs. Davis
said.

"I know. I heard about his accident, and I'm,
um, I'm so sorry."

Mrs. Davis closed her eyes, remembering. "It
was the most horrible thing imaginable, getting

that call." She opened her eyes again, staring straight at Cassie.

Cassie opened her mouth to say something, but Mrs. Davis continued. "The kids were on their way to a party. It was such a foggy night. Ethan's friend James was driving. I always warned my Ethan not to drink and drive, and he was so careful about it. But James—he'd started drinking before they even left his house. His girlfriend couldn't make it to the dance, and he was angry with her—and determined to have a good time." She shook her head sadly.

"I got the call at 10:05 P.M. I'll never forget it. All the officer said was, 'Mrs. Davis? I'm calling about your son.' And I knew. I just knew he was gone." She dabbed at her eyes with a yellowing silk napkin from the tray. "They found James's car wrapped around a tree out on Route 7. No one survived."

Cassie didn't know what to say. "Sorry" seemed so inadequate. She reached out and put her hand on Mrs. Davis's arm.

Suddenly, Mrs. Davis's eyes brightened. "But you're here now, aren't you?"

Cassie nodded slowly, not sure how her being here helped anything.

"Would you like to go up to his room?" Mrs. Davis asked.

"Um, sure." She still was no closer to finding out who was texting her or their connection to Ethan Davis. Maybe his room would reveal some clues.

Mrs. Davis led her up the curved staircase. Along the wall were pictures of the Davis family in much happier times—Ethan dressed in a ski jacket and standing at the top of a slope, Mr. and Mrs. Davis on their wedding day (Cassie was right, she had been beautiful), and Ethan as a little boy, holding on to his father's hand as they fed the ducks at Lake Pinquot.

At the top of the stairs, Mrs. Davis turned right and led Cassie to a closed door. Slowly Mrs. Davis opened it, and they stepped inside. If the living room looked like a museum, Ethan's bedroom was like a time capsule. It was as though everything had stopped the very second he died. His bed was still made. The walls were covered in posters of bands from the eighties, some of which Cassie recognized—The Cure, The Smiths, The Alarm, and Depeche Mode. The shelves were filled with books, including, Cassie noticed, a copy of *The Catcher in the Rye.*

Mrs. Davis walked over to the bookshelf and reached up to where two identical yearbooks sat. She pulled one off the shelf. It looked exactly like the one Elise had showed Cassie the other day at the school office. Then Mrs. Davis opened the book, rifling through the dog-eared pages. After a few seconds, she showed the book to Cassie. There was the now-familiar picture of Ethan. Under the picture was signed, "To Cassandra. Love, Ethan."

Mrs. Davis turned some more pages. When she stopped, she put her finger on a picture of a girl. Underneath her picture was a name— Cassandra Mason. Cassie stared for a minute at this girl from the past. She took in Cassandra's frizzy auburn hair and big eyes. Cassandra had high cheeks and lips that curled up slightly at the edges. Her pointed chin made her face look heart-shaped. She looked exactly like Cassie.

Mrs. Davis looked up at Cassie. "When you and Ethan died in that car accident, it was like I died too. Welcome back, Cassandra."

Cassie closed the front door behind her a lot harder than she had intended. The sound sent her mother running out of her home office, a freshly sharpened pencil still tucked behind one ear. "Cassie? Is that you?"

Cassie tried to catch her breath enough to answer calmly. "Yes, Mom. Sorry, I didn't mean to slam the door."

"Why are you panting?"

"I walked home really fast." It was a terrible lie.

"Then why did I see Steve's car pulling out of our driveway just now?"

Cassie sighed. She kept forgetting that her mother's office had a bird's-eye view of the driveway (which was something she'd definitely have to remember if she was ever lucky enough to get a date).

"What's wrong? Tell me." Her mother was giving her "the look"—probably the same look evil dictators gave before they tortured people into telling the truth.

Cassie couldn't look her mother in the eye. "Well, you know that guy who's been calling me? Ethan?"

Her mother nodded. Cassie could tell her mother was holding back from saying, *I told you we should have gotten the police involved.*

"I checked with Elise to find out whether there's anyone by that name at Bridgewater, and the only person who matched his picture was . . ."

"Yes?"

"Ethan Davis—who died twenty-five years ago," Cassie whispered. Her mother's eyes widened. "I found out where his mom used to live, and Jen, Steve, and I drove over there today." She looked at her mom, trying to figure out whether she was about to be grounded until college.

Then the rest of the story tumbled out of her. "His mom showed me Ethan's room—his yearbook. There was a picture of him and a girl named Cassandra, his girlfriend. She died with him in the car accident. Mom—she looked exactly like me. And Mrs. Davis said, 'Welcome back, Cassandra.' Like I was *her*. She looked at me like I had come back from the dead."

Her mother drew in her breath sharply. Then she dropped her head. A tear ran down her cheek.

"Mom! What's wrong?"

Cassie's mother looked up at her, visibly shaken but trying to keep it together. "Cassie was my best friend growing up. You were named after her. And you do look so much like her. Sometimes when I look at you, I feel like she's still here."

"Mom! Are you serious? Why didn't you ever tell me that? I thought you plucked my name out of one of your favorite novels!"

"No." Her mom smiled sadly. "Cassie and I had been friends since the third grade. We did everything together—learned how to ride bikes, went double on our first dates, drove to Boston to see The Cure in concert. Right before graduation, we were supposed to go to a party with her boyfriend, Ethan Davis, and James, the guy I was dating. I was ice-skating competitively back then—remember how I told you I won the state championship back in 1985?"

Cassie nodded. Her mom had been one of the best young skaters in the state until her freshman year in college, when a bad fall had forced her to drop out of the sport. Cassie was not similarly blessed in the athletic department. She could barely stagger onto the ice without falling.

"The championship was the day after the party," Cassie's mom continued. "I didn't want to be up late the night before a big competition, so I stayed home. James was really angry with me. I guess he had too much to drink before he, Ethan, and Cassie went to the party, and he got behind the wheel drunk." She paused to wipe her nose with a tissue from her pocket. "None of them made it."

"Why didn't you ever tell me about it?"

"It's hard for me to talk about, Cassie. I've felt so guilty since then."

"Guilty? For what?"

"For not being in the car. For being the one who lived."

"But Mom, it's not your fault James was drinking and driving."

"I know, but I kept thinking that if I had been there, maybe he wouldn't have been drinking. Or maybe I could have talked him out of driving." Cassie's mom tilted her head slightly to one side and surveyed her daughter.

"Cassie was such a beautiful person. Just like you. It still breaks my heart that she's gone."

"I'm sorry you lost your best friend, Mom," Cassie said. "But why do you think Mrs. Davis acted so weird when I came over? She had to have known that I wasn't the same Cassie who died."

"Cassie, she lost her son in a horrible car accident. She's probably still heartbroken, even after all these years. Losing a child has got to be the most painful experience imaginable. Maybe you looked so much like Ethan's girlfriend that you brought back all those memories."

"I guess. It was just so weird, the way she looked at me."

"Mrs. Davis is a lonely old woman, Cassie. First she lost her child, then her husband. She's just trying to hold on to anything that reminds her of Ethan."

"Yeah. I guess you're right. Now I feel horrible."

"Why?"

"She spooked me so much that I ran out of her house. I didn't even say good-bye."

"Why don't you go back and apologize? Tell her that you didn't know the whole story, and now you do. It might do Mrs. Davis some good to talk with you."

"Good idea. I'll go back this weekend."

"Great. And promise me something, Cassie?"

"What?"

"Never, ever drink and drive or drive with anyone who has been drinking."

It wasn't the first time her mother had given her this advice, but it was the first time Cassie didn't shrug it off.

"I promise," she said, nodding solemnly.

So you're really going back?" Jen asked between sit-ups.

"Yeah," Cassie replied. "I still haven't got a clue about who's been texting me, and don't you think I should apologize for running out of her house? . . . Hey, stop squirming so much. I can barely hold onto your feet."

"Sorry," Jen said, slowing down a little. "You did run out of there like you were possessed. And when you yelled at Steve to 'Floor it!'

I thought you were being chased by a mobster or serial killer." Her voice got progressively louder. From across the gym, Mrs. Wilson glared at them.

"Shhhh," Cassie whispered. "If we get detention, I won't be able to go over to Mrs. Davis's this afternoon."

"Are you sure you don't want Steve and me to take you over there again?"

"Nah, she's harmless. A little weird maybe—but harmless. I think she just misses her son."

"Are you still getting the texts?"

"Yep. Four this morning alone. But now he just keeps writing the same two things—'Help me' and 'Come home.'"

"Maybe your dead boyfriend's already run out of things to say to you."

"Very funny. And would you stop calling him that? Obviously, Ethan Davis isn't texting me from the grave. It has to be someone punking me."

A shadow loomed over Cassie and Jen. "You ladies seem to have a lot to talk about when you should be working out." Mrs. Wilson raised her whistle to her lips. "I think a little detention might cure those overactive mouths of yours."

"Oh please, no, Mrs. Wilson," Cassie pleaded. "Today is the day I help out the kids at the foster home after school. Little Jennie will be so heartbroken if I'm not there. She so looks forward to my visits." She looked up forlornly.

Mrs. Wilson lowered her whistle, and for the first time ever, Cassie saw a glimpse of something that looked almost like humanity cross her gym teacher's face. "Well, I guess we wouldn't want to upset the children. No detention today, but let this be a warning to you," she said, pointing one finger at the girls. "Now give me twenty."

Both girls quickly jumped into push-up position and started pumping their arms.

As Mrs. Wilson walked away, Jen whispered, "Good one, Cass. Good luck today. Call me as soon as you've talked to Mrs. Davis."

"I will."

"And make sure to say hello for me to those poor kids at the foster home."

Cassie rested all her body weight on one hand. With the other hand she reached over and smacked her friend on the shoulder.

Cassie rode her bike over to Mrs. Davis's house. Even though she was seventeen, her mother wouldn't let her have a car. Cassie used to complain about that. Now, at least, she knew where her mom was coming from.

As she walked up the now-familiar path to the front door, Cassie worried. What if Mrs. Davis was angry at her for running out the other day? Now that Cassie knew the whole story about Ethan, her actions seemed especially rude. And would she be able to get the information she needed out of Mrs. Davis, who was still so obviously grieving over her long-dead son?

Cassie worried, but she kept walking. She knew she had to go back, both to apologize and to learn more about Ethan.

Hesitantly, Cassie reached for the lion door knocker. Before she could let it go, the door swung open, nearly taking Cassie's hand with it. Mrs. Davis was standing there. This time, her hair was done in some kind of elegant updo, and she was wearing glossy red lipstick and clumpy mascara. She was wearing a bright blue jumpsuit with a white collar and white elastic cuffs. She looked at least ten years younger.

Mrs. Davis's arms were extended. She was giving Cassie a welcoming smile. "Cassie, my dear! I'm so glad you decided to come back."

"Mrs. Davis, I am so sorry for my behavior the last time I was here."

"Nonsense," Mrs. Davis brushed aside her

apology with a now-manicured hand and ushered Cassie inside. "I came on way too strong, taking you up to Ethan's room and showing you that yearbook. I just hope I didn't frighten you too much."

"I did get a little spooked," Cassie admitted as Mrs. Davis shut the front door behind her. "But I was so rude to just run out like that. My mother explained everything to me, so now I understand."

"Wonderful! So, would it be all right if we continue our tea?" Mrs. Davis motioned to the living room. Today the room looked brand-new. All of the surfaces were sparkling clean, and the vase held fresh roses. On the coffee table sat a tea set with two teacups and a plate of sugar cookies.

"Sure," Cassie said, although she did think it was a little strange that the tea was already set up. Could her mother have somehow called Mrs. Davis to tell her she was coming? Or maybe Mrs. Davis had been expecting someone else this afternoon?

"I realize that I come on too strong sometimes," Mrs. Davis said as they picked up their teacups. The tea was still steaming hot. "But I'm just an old, lonely woman." Mrs. Davis gave Cassie a sad smile. "Sometimes I forget how to act around company."

As they drank their tea, Mrs. Davis reminisced about happier times. She told Cassie about their first family vacation at Stowe Mountain Resort in Vermont when Ethan was just six years old. It was Ethan's first time on skis, and he ended up sliding most of the way down the bunny slope on his behind. "You should have seen the look of surprise on his little face!" Mrs. Davis exclaimed.

"It sounds like something I would have done," Cassie said, laughing.

"Oh no, you're much more coordinated than that," said Mrs. Davis. There she went again, acting like she knew Cassie. It was probably like her mom had said. Mrs. Davis missed her son so much that she wanted to hold on to anything that had to do with him, including his high school girlfriend.

After a few more stories—including Ethan's spectacular win in the third-grade spelling bee—Mrs. Davis put down her teacup. "I don't want to upset you, Cassie, but there is something else I'd really like to show you. Something that I think will answer the questions you've been having."

Cassie didn't want to hurt the woman's feelings, and she thought maybe Mrs. Davis would have something to tell her about the text messages. "Sure," she said. She let the older woman lead her through the kitchen. They came to an old, scratched door that was falling off its hinges. Mrs. Davis yanked it open.

"Watch your step. I'm afraid these basement stairs have gone into disrepair since my husband passed away," Mrs. Davis said.

The stairs creaked and groaned as

Cassie followed Mrs. Davis into the gloomy basement. The smell of mold and wet earth was overpowering, and Cassie coughed to stop from gagging. Cobwebs brushed Cassie's cheeks. Instinctively, she raised her arms, grazing the wet, crumbling walls with her fingers.

Something was glowing from below. When she got to the bottom of the stairs and rounded the corner, Cassie saw the source of the light—candles, dozens of them, all over a long, wooden table. Cassie waited for her eyes to adjust. At first all she could see were tall, slanting shadows. Then she made out rows and rows of rectangles. Cassie got closer. The rectangles were picture frames. Cassie gasped. Every one showed Ethan.

Ethan as a baby in his mother's arms. Toddler Ethan running through a sprinkler. Ethan, in elementary school, in a plaid shirt and showing a gap-toothed smile. Most of them showed the Ethan that Cassie knew best. Teenaged Ethan in a powder-blue tuxedo with a white carnation boutonniere. Then Ethan, same outfit, with Cassandra in pink ruffles. Ethan in a baseball uniform. *It was a shrine to Ethan.*

C assie knew she should run, but she couldn't help edging in closer. Something was on the table's faded surface. A phone!

"I've been having such a hard time learning how to use that thing—you know, at my age, computers, cell phones—they're such a chore." Cassie spun around to face Mrs. Davis. The woman's glossy lips were stretched into a strange grimace. "I had so hoped you would come back, Cassie."

Mrs. Davis leaned forward so that her face was just inches away from Cassie's. The old woman smelled like baby powder, tea, and decay all at once. Cassie turned away, but Mrs. Davis caught the edge of her chin and swiveled it back to face her own. "And now you're here. Everything is unfolding just perfectly." She sang the words a little, grinning widely at her little performance. Cassie noticed a row of black holes in the back of her mouth where her teeth had rotted away.

"What are you planning?" Cassie whispered.

"I've brought you back, and now we're going to bring Ethan back . . . together." Mrs. Davis grabbed one of Cassie's arms and twisted it behind her back. With a cry, Cassie fell to her knees, Mrs. Davis standing behind her.

"Ethan's dead!" Cassie shouted. "He's never coming back—"

"Shut up!" Cassie felt her head snap back as Mrs. Davis pulled on her hair. Then Mrs. Davis's shadow fell across the front of her body. Cassie caught the glint of a long needle in the edge of her vision. It dripped once on her cheek. Then she felt a prick in her upper arm.

Cassie wanted to yell. She wanted to throw up her arms and push Mrs. Davis off her. But she couldn't move. Her muscles felt heavy; her tongue felt like lead. Then Mrs. Davis was there in front of her, her blue-and-white image all wavy, like heat coming off pavement. *She . . . drugged . . . me.* The words formed in Cassie's head. Then everything went black.

A dead spider. That was the next thing Cassie saw. Inches from her face and covered in dust. Normally Cassie was terrified of bugs, but right now she was too terrified of other things. Her mouth felt like it had been stuffed with cotton, and her head ached. Then there were her wrists and ankles. It was like they were on fire. *Rope,* Cassie realized. She was tied up, arms behind her back.

Cassie pushed one shoulder against the wall. But without the help of her arms, she couldn't push herself up. *Slam!* She fell back, banging the back of her head on the cement floor.

"Why?" Cassie heard her own voice talking, and she took it as a good sign. Fear had made her stupid, but at least her brain still wanted to think. Why hadn't she taken Jen up on her offer? Why had she come to this place alone?

This time Cassie did a sit-up to thrust her body into a sitting position. A line of faded candlelight seeped under the door. Cassie could just make out the fake-wood siding of whatever kind of closet she was in. Her feet were already by the door. *Good.* Cassie pushed against the door as hard as she could, but it didn't bend or even creak. Cassie brought her legs up and tried slamming them down at an angle. The impact made a kind of ringing sound.

The irony didn't escape her: everything else in this old basement was crumbling and broken, but Mrs. Davis had managed to install a top-of-the-line steel door for Cassie's prison cell.

What would Mrs. Davis do to her? Could she—would she actually kill her?

Footsteps echoed behind the door. Mrs. Davis was out there! Cassie turned her body around so that her head was by the door. She peered through the crack, but all she could see was the dark-light-dark-light pattern that Mrs. Davis made as she passed back and forth.

Cassie shut her eyes. For a second, she heard a splashing sound. Then, for several minutes, a long, slow scraping. Mrs. Davis was talking too. Was someone else there? Maybe the person she'd been expecting for tea?

Cassie put her head on the floor.

"It's okay, Ethan. Mommy's coming." Okay, that made sense. Crazy Mrs. Davis was making baby talk to her dead son.

"Mommy's missed you so much."

Cassie cringed.

"I know it was her fault, Ethan. I know you didn't want to go to that party. She made you. I know it, my sweet boy. YOU were always such a good boy, staying by your Mommy's side . . ."

"What the hell?" Cassie couldn't help saying it out loud. Mrs. Davis's level of craziness was reaching new heights.

". . . until that evil girl!" No more sweet talk now. "But she's going to pay!" Cassie heard a bang like a pounding fist, then objects clattering. A long silence and then a gasp—a sob? "She *will* pay, Ethan." Whispering now. "With her very flesh."

Cassie thought that she had known fear before this. When she'd been lost in the woods at summer camp, when she'd made it to the top of the climbing wall at the gym, at her first funeral with a real dead body—Cassie thought she'd been afraid then. But no. That was nothing like this. Now, fear was like a creature inside her, sucking her insides into a hole in the middle of her stomach. This fear made her shake with hot and cold at the same time. It made the blackness around her seep under her skin.

⁕

Click. A lock was turning. Then, light. Mrs. Davis was standing in the open door.

"Well, my dear." She smiled broadly. "I hope you had a nice nap. You're going to need your strength for what's ahead."

"You can't keep me here," Cassie spat out at her captor. "My mother knows exactly where I am, and when I don't come home this afternoon, she's going to have the police over here right away."

Mrs. Davis didn't seem the least bit flustered by that bit of information. "Oh, we'll be long done by then, Cassandra."

She grabbed Cassie's right arm and dragged her out of the closet. A wave of pain shot through Cassie's elbow. It was the one she'd cracked by falling out of a tree when she was seven. "Ow!" Cassie screamed.

"Oh be quiet!" Mrs. Davis slapped her across the face. Tears sprang from Cassie's eyes. No one had ever hit her before.

Then, the woman's voice softened. "Oh, I'm sorry, sweetie." She stroked Cassie's cheek with one finger. She reminded Cassie of a cat toying with its prey. "Just behave, and everything will go smoothly. You'll see."

Mrs. Davis pulled her into the room, where the candles still burned in front of the shrine to Ethan. Cassie tried to hold in the sobs that squeezed her throat. Frantically, she tried to hop to her feet.

Mrs. Davis pushed her back down with the heel of her shoe. "When I say behave, I mean do as I say." Cassie noticed for the first time that Mrs. Davis was holding one arm behind her back. Now she brought it forward. A butcher knife was clenched in her fist.

Cassie's eyes widened. Now she knew for sure. She was going to die in here.

Mrs. Davis looked down at the knife and

then back up at Cassie. A small, wicked smile played around her lips. "Impressive, isn't it? I've become something of a knife connoisseur since my husband died. Sitting at home all day, there's not much to do but order things from QVC—like kitchen knife sets." She held up one finger and lightly touched the end of the blade to it. Immediately, a drop of blood welled up.

"I was just sharpening it during your little nap. It's *very* sharp."

"You're crazy," Cassie whispered, shrinking backward as far from Mrs. Davis as possible.

"Crazy like a fox, as they say!" Mrs. Davis cackled, revealing those black holes again. "I've lived without my Ethan for twenty-five years. Now, with your help, he's finally going to come back to me."

"What are you going to do?" Cassie's heart was pounding so loudly in her chest that she worried she might faint.

Mrs. Davis raised a finger on her free hand. "Ah yes, my plan! You see, I did some research at the Bridgewater library, and I've learned so much. So much! I found an old book on witchcraft. Do you want to know what was in it?"

Cassie gave the tiniest reluctant nod.

"An ancient potion to bring back a loved one from beyond!" In her excitement, Mrs. Davis squeezed the knife, releasing a spray of blood from her finger. She didn't seem to notice. "But I needed ingredients. Yes, I did." Another gleeful laugh. "Acacia leaves, holy water, candles, a bowl bearing the symbol of Osiris—Egyptian god of the underworld." Mrs. Davis paused, motioning to the altar behind her on which all of these items were now carefully displayed. Then she turned back to Cassie. "And flesh."

Cassie shrank back even farther. This was a nightmare. It had to be. There was no way she was really here with this insane woman.

"But not just any flesh," Mrs. Davis continued. "Oh no. It had to be the flesh of someone close to my Ethan." She leaned forward and slid the cool blade against Cassie's cheek. "*Your* flesh."

Mrs. Davis pulled Cassie onto a chair and stood behind her. Then she grabbed a coil of rope from a wooden crate by her feet. Round and round, she wrapped up Cassie's upper body, pinning it to the top of the chair but leaving her arms free.

With one slice, Mrs. Davis cut the ropes around Cassie's wrists. Immediately, Cassie brought her arms around in front of her. She gasped at the welts, bloody bracelets around her wrists.

Mrs. Davis held her knife in front of her like a bridal bouquet.

This is it, Cassie thought. *This is how my life is going to end. In a dirty basement, killed by a crazy woman.*

But Mrs. Davis wasn't done yet. "Now for our next activity!" she said brightly. "The question is—whose turn is it?" She held the knife out to Cassie. "Yours or mine?" That black-gapped smile again. "Now, where are my manners? Of course. Guests first!" Mrs. Davis placed the knife in Cassie's hands.

For several seconds, Mrs. Davis and Cassie both stared at the knife shaking in Cassie's hands.

"For goodness' sake!" Mrs. Davis snapped. "Don't make me come over there and do it for you!"

"Do . . . what?" Cassie whispered. She was crying now, either out of fear or anger, or both.

Mrs. Davis made a fake frown. "Why, cut! Cut, Cassandra. Cut your flesh. My spell calls for 'a coin-sized piece of flesh' . . . " Mrs. Davis laughed in anticipation of her own joke. "Let's be on the safe side, and make it at least a quarter!"

Suddenly, "Use Somebody" was playing from inside Cassie's jeans pocket. Her phone! She'd forgotten she still had it with her.

Cassie threw the knife across the room and, with her freed hands, reached for the phone. Confusion flashed over Mrs. Davis's face. For a second she stood motionless as she wondered whether to lunge for the phone or the knife.

As Cassie fumbled for the phone, Mrs. Davis ran for the knife. By the time Cassie had managed to free the phone from her pocket, Mrs. Davis was back. She raised her arm, lifting the knife up above her head. "I was trying to do this nicely, but *obviously* you are not going to cooperate."

Just then a deafening noise, like rushing water, filled the room. The knife swung toward Cassie, and she dropped the phone.

Everything came fast now. A bright,

blinding flash. Glass shattering, as if someone had thrown a large rock through a window. A burst of wind blowing out the candles. The ropes around Cassie's chest and legs unraveling in the air around her.

Mrs. Davis stood her ground, pointing the knife at Cassie's chest. Then another huge gust of wind blasted, and the knife was gone. The weapon seemed to blow right out of Mrs. Davis's clenched fist. And the wind that took it seemed to whisper, "She's mine."

The knife clattered to the floor. Now it was pitch black, except for the screen of Cassie's phone. Cassie lunged for it and quickly punched in 911. She could hear Mrs. Davis scrambling around on the floor, grabbing for the knife.

"911. What's the emergency?"

"Help me! This crazy woman is trying to kill me!" Cassie screamed.

"Who is trying to kill you? Where are you?" the operator asked.

"Don't you dare call anyone!" Mrs. Davis

growled from the floor just a few feet from her. Cassie scrambled away from Mrs. Davis's voice. She tried to run in the direction of the stairs. Feeling blindly along the damp, crumbling walls, she hit something with her foot—the bottom stair.

Then she was on her knees, winded. Mrs. Davis was on top of her, pounding at her back with her fists. "You are not going anywhere! You *will* help me get my Ethan back!" she screamed.

The phone slipped out of Cassie's grasp. "Hello? Hello? Is anyone there?" the operator asked.

Mrs. Davis kicked the phone away from Cassie's outstretched hand.

Cassie had never had to fight before. She had no idea what to do. She thrust her arms out in every direction and kicked her legs like a wild animal. She felt the blunt force of Mrs. Davis's fists against her back, legs, and chest.

Finally, the blows stopped. Cassie's back

and neck ached. Her head felt like it was stuffed with cotton. Again she tried to reach for her phone. But when she lifted her body up on her arms, the room started spinning. For the second time that afternoon, everything went black.

A bright light was shining down on her. *Is this the light people describe when they have a near-death experience?* Cassie wondered. *Am I dead?*

But she hurt way too much to be dead. Her arms ached. Her back throbbed. And her mouth felt dry and pasty.

"There's someone down here!" she heard a man call from above. The light went away for a second. When it returned, it was followed by footsteps on the creaky basement stairs.

Cassie tried to sit up. "Take it easy there, miss. We're here to help you." An officer was at her side, assisting her. But where was Mrs. Davis?

"There's someone else over here! An older woman," said another officer, who was shining his flashlight around the room. "She looks like she's been knocked unconscious."

"She—she tried to kill me!" Cassie said, and the sobs broke free. She sat on the basement floor, her chest heaving, for what felt like several minutes.

"It's okay," the officer who was propping her up said reassuringly. "We'll get your story in a minute. First we need to make sure everyone's okay."

Cassie could hear the other officer calling for medical assistance on his two-way radio. A few minutes later, a couple of EMTs came down the stairs holding a stretcher. They loaded Mrs. Davis onto it. Now she was moaning, "Ethan. My sweet Ethan. Why did you stop me? We could have been together again!"

By the time the second stretcher arrived, Cassie had calmed down. The EMT asked her to lie down on it, but she shook her head. Even though her body ached, she didn't think anything was broken. The last thing she wanted was to go to the hospital. She just wanted to get home.

The EMT quickly checked her over and put a Band-Aid on her cheek. Once she got up the stairs and outside, one of the officers asked her a series of questions about what had happened. Cassie answered every one, while the other officer called her mother to come pick her up.

Suddenly, Cassie realized she'd left her cell phone in Mrs. Davis's basement. "Officer?" she asked tentatively. "Would it be okay if I go back down there for just a second? I really need to get my phone."

The officer shook his head. "I'm afraid I can't let you do that," he said apologetically.

"I'll just be a second. Please? And I'll take the flashlight."

"No can do, Cassie. Just hang here. In a minute I'll send someone in to get your phone for you."

The officer went back over to the ambulance, where a few of his fellow officers were conferring over the outstretched form of Mrs. Davis. She was still moaning about her Ethan.

When the officer didn't return after a few minutes or look her way, Cassie decided to go back after her phone herself. She grabbed a flashlight that had been left on the roof of a patrol car and sneaked around to the back of the house. There, at basement level, a window had been shattered.

She used a rock to break the rest of the glass. When the window was clear, she shimmied through it. It was a short drop to the basement floor.

Picking her way around the glass shards, Cassie aimed her flashlight at the floor. It was covered in candle wax and dust. She pointed the flashlight at the shrine on the wall. Ethan smiled at her from hundreds of different angles.

"I could have liked you," Cassie said softly. She ran her finger along the edge of a photo of Ethan lying on the beach. "I liked you liking me." *How sad that the whole thing was the twisted invention of a crazy old woman,* Cassie thought.

Yet she still had two big unanswered questions. First, how did Mrs. Davis get her cell-phone number? And second, what had happened to make Mrs. Davis stop attacking her?

Cassie's flashlight stopped on something glowing on the floor. It was her cell phone, still lying open where she had dropped it. Cassie picked it up and looked at the screen. It read, "1 new text message." That must have been the message that came in when she had dropped her phone.

Cassie clicked on the envelope icon. The number was all too familiar.

Don't go. I love you.

A cool breeze tickled the back of her neck. It felt like a kiss. Then it started to get warmer. It burned.

The wind blew harder. Broken glass started skittering around the floor. Upstairs, the basement door started slamming. The shutters on the windows started flapping too.

Her phone was ringing again. Another text. *I saved your life. You're all mine now.*

Now something was happening in the bowl of holy water. Cassie tentatively stepped closer. Words were appearing.

Together forever.

The words looked like they were written in blood.

Cassie wasn't about to make the same mistake twice. With all the strength left in her aching body, she ran up the stairs, through the slamming basement door, and out into the sunlight of the fall afternoon.

Wow! It sounds like the plot of some crazy horror movie!" Jen was looking at her wide-eyed over the lunch table.

Lisa nodded vigorously over her half-finished chocolate shake. "I can't believe some guy's ghost fell in love with you! And you fought off that crazy, knife-wielding lunatic! You're like an action movie star! Like Jackie Chan!" She did an exaggerated karate chop.

"Nah," Cassie shrugged. Yet she had felt a

little like a celebrity at school that morning. Just about everyone had heard what had happened to her at the Davis house. It had even made the front page of the *Bridgewater Gazette* (although a Little League win could also make front page in this small town). Students had come up to her in the hallway, asking her about what had happened. A couple of freshmen had even asked for her autograph.

"Hey, Cassie, I have some good news and some bad news," Jen said, smiling.

Cassie groaned. Not again. "This time, why don't you give me the bad news first?"

"Jonah's on his way over here to congratulate you on your heroics." She motioned behind Cassie.

Without turning around, Cassie asked, "And what's the good news?"

Jen raised her eyebrows. "See for yourself!"

Cassie looked up to see Jonah approaching their table. When she turned back to Liz and Jen, she saw them grabbing what was left of their lunches and slipping away from the table. She mouthed, "Guys! What are you—" And then Jonah was standing next to her.

This was not the Jonah who Cassie had met at the flagpole before Halloween. First, he'd gotten his braces taken off. His teeth were white and perfect. It also looked like he'd picked out his own clothes, for once. He was wearing faded skinny jeans with a dark blue sweater. She had to admit, he looked good.

"Hey, Cassie. I heard what happened to you this weekend. Crazy stuff." He shook his head. "I'm really glad you're okay." Having his braces off must have given Jonah a newfound confidence, because he didn't stumble at all this time.

"Thanks, Jonah. I am too. It got a little hairy there for a minute." She'd never noticed before how blue his eyes were.

"Listen, I know I haven't had much luck in talking to you over these last few weeks, but I've been really wanting to ask you out. Do you want to go out to a movie or have dinner with me sometime?"

A few weeks ago she would have found some excuse. But in that period of time everything in her world had been turned upside down. Why not go out with him?

"Sure, Jonah. I'd love to go out with you."

"That's great! Can I get your cell phone number? Or give you mine?"

"I thought your mother didn't let you have a cell phone."

"My mother and I have been having some discussions lately about what a seventeen-year-old should be allowed to do. I think she's finally coming around." He smiled. He had a great smile.

Cassie smiled back. Then she scribbled her number down on a napkin and handed it to Jonah.

"I'll call you after school," he said. "If you're done with lunch, do you want to go outside and hang out on the lawn before sixth period?"

"That sounds great." Cassie picked the remnants of her lunch off the table. As she threw them out, she saw Jen giving her a big thumbs-up from across the room.

Cassie followed Jonah out the door of the cafeteria. From her purse, she could hear the sounds of "Use Somebody" drifting up from her cell phone.

Cassie grabbed the cell phone and hurled it into a trash can. She'd have to let Jonah know— she was definitely getting a new phone number.

Everything's fine in Bridgewater. Really...

Or is it?

Look for these other titles from the
Night Fall collection.

THE CLUB

The club started innocently enough. Bored after school, Josh and his friends decided to try out an old game Sabina had found in her basement. Called "Black Magic," it promised the players good fortune at the expense of those who have wronged them. Yeah, right.

But when the club members' luck starts skyrocketing—and horror befalls their enemies—the game stops being a joke. How can they end the power they've unleashed? Answers lie in an old diary—but ending the game may be deadlier than any curse.

THE PROTECTORS

Luke's life has never been "normal." How could it be, with his mother holding séances and his half-crazy stepfather working as Bridgewater's mortician? But living in a funeral home never bothered Luke. That is, until the night of his mom's accident.

Sounds of screaming now shatter Luke's dreams. And his stepfather is acting even stranger. When bodies in the funeral home start delivering messages to Luke, he is certain that he's going nuts. As he tries to solve his mother's death, Luke discovers a secret more horrifying than any nightmare.

SKIN

It looks like a pizza exploded on Nick Barry's face. But bad skin is the least of his problems. His bones feel like living ice. A strange rash—like scratches—seems to be some sort of ancient code. And then there's the anger . . .

Something evil is living under Nick's skin. Where did it come from? What does it want? With the help of a dead kid's diary, a nun, and a local professor, Nick slowly finds out what's wrong with him. But there's still one question that Nick must face alone: How do you destroy an evil that's inside you?

THAW

A July storm caused a major power outage in Bridgewater. Now a research project at the Institute for Cryogenic Experimentation has been ruined, and the thawed-out bodies of twenty-seven federal inmates are missing.

At first, Dani Kraft didn't think much of the breaking news. But after her best friend Jake disappears, a mysterious visitor connects the dots for Dani. Jake has been taken in by an infamous cult leader. To get him back, Dani must enter a dangerous alternate reality where a defrosted cult leader is beginning to act like some kind of god.

UNTHINKABLE

Omar Phillips is Bridgewater High's favorite local teen author. His Facebook fans can't wait for his next horror story. But lately Omar's imagination has turned against him. Horrifying visions of death and destruction come over him with wide-screen intensity. The only way to stop the visions is to write them down. Until they start coming true . . .

Enter Sophie Minax, the mysterious Goth girl who's been following Omar at school. "I'm one of you," Sophie says. She tells Omar how to end the visions—but the only thing worse than Sophie's cure may be what happens if he ignores it.